DAVID WIESNER

The Loathsome Dragon

RETOLD BY DAVID WIESNER & KIM KAHNG

CLARION BOOKS • NEW YORK

THIS STORY WAS RETOLD by British folklorist Joseph Jacobs in *English Fairy Tales*, 1890, as "The Laidly Worm of Spindleston Heugh." It was based on an eighteenth-century ballad, and Jacobs speculated that the ballad's original hero, Owain (or Owein), was the same character as Sir Gawain of Arthurian legend. I found the image of the maiden awakening in her bed as a "laidly worm," or loathsome dragon, so striking that I painted it as a poster for The Original Art, an exhibition of children's book illustration, in 1985. And then I thought of retelling and illustrating the whole story. My wife, Kim Kahng, and I have freely adapted Jacobs's version for the picture-book format and audience.

D. W.

Thanks to Every Picture Tells a Story.

Clarion Books
a Houghton Mifflin Company imprint
215 Park Avenue South, New York, NY 10003
Copyright © 1987, 2005 by David Wiesner and Kim Kahng
The text was set in 14.5-point ITC Golden Cockerel.
The illustrations were executed in watercolor.
Calligraphy by Paul Shaw. Book design by Carol Goldenberg.
www.houghtonmifflinbooks.com
Printed in the U.S.A.

Library of Congress Cataloging-in-Publication Data

Wiesner, David.
The loathsome dragon / retold by David Wiesner and Kim Kahng ; illustrated by David Wiesner.
p. cm.
Summary: A wicked queen casts a spell over her beautiful stepdaughter, turning her into a loathsome dragon until such time as her wandering brother shall return and kiss her three times.
ISBN 0-618-54359-7
[1. Fairy tales. 2. Folklore—England. 3. Dragons—Folklore.] I. Kahng, Kim. II. Title.
PZ8.1.W638Lo 2005
398.2—dc22
2004018759

ISBN-13: 978-0-618-54359-5
ISBN-10: 0-618-54359-7

WOZ 10 9 8 7 6 5 4 3

For Mom & Dad —D.W.

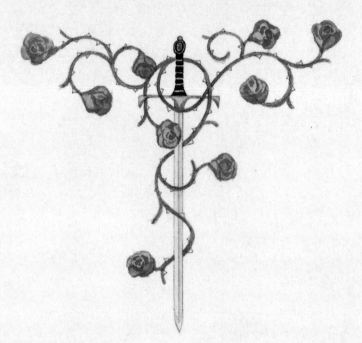

For Kevin & Jaime —K.U.K.

In Bamborough Castle there lived a king and queen who had a son named Richard and a daughter named Margaret. Both children were as fair as a summer's morning and grew up to be as kind and brave as they were beautiful. In time, Richard set off to see the world. Soon after, the queen died. For several years, the king had only his sorrow and his daughter for company. Then one day, while he was away hunting, he met a beautiful enchantress. Bewitched, he fell instantly in love with her and sent word to Margaret that he was bringing home a new queen.

Princess Margaret was startled to hear that she would soon have a stepmother, but she was pleased that her father seemed so happy. She arranged an elegant reception for the arrival of her father and his bride. With a graceful curtsy, Margaret presented the new queen with the keys to the castle. Watching the king gaze at his daughter with obvious pride, the queen burned with jealousy. "We'll see just how well-loved this child remains," she hissed.

That very night the queen stole silently to the dungeon, and there in the darkness she wove her magic. Nine times nine she passed her arms before herself, and three times three she chanted her evil spell.

> *Change love to fear, princess to dragon,*
> *Forevermore shall this be,*
> *Unless Prince Richard, the king's own son,*
> *Gives the beast kisses three.*

And so it was that Margaret went to sleep a fair princess and awoke the next morning a Loathsome Dragon.

The dragon slithered from its bed and crawled out of the castle. It scaled the steep hillside to a giant rock called the Spindle Stone. There it lay for a time, but soon enough it began to roam the kingdom, devouring everything in its path.

The people were terrified, and they asked a mighty wizard how to rid themselves of this dreadful creature. After consulting his books and scrolls of magic, the wizard told them, "The Loathsome Dragon is Princess Margaret bewitched, and it is hunger that drives her forth. Put aside seven cows, and as the sun goes down each day, carry every drop of milk they yield to the trough that lies at the foot of the Spindle Stone. The milk will satisfy her, and she will leave you alone. But if you wish to break the spell and punish the one who bewitched her, send over the seas for her brother. Prince Richard alone can save his sister—and he must do so within a year, or she will remain a dragon forever."

All was done as the wizard advised. The people sent a message
to Prince Richard, and each day they fed the Loathsome Dragon
the milk of seven cows, so that it troubled the kingdom no longer.

Months passed before the message finally reached Prince Richard. The moment he heard of Princess Margaret's fate, he swore a mighty oath that he would rescue her and take vengeance upon the enchantress who had cast the spell. Three and thirty of his men took the oath with him. They built a ship with a keel made of magic rowan wood, and when all was ready, they set sail for Bamborough Castle.

Now, when the queen learned of Prince Richard's approach, she flew into a rage. "He shall never reach the shore!" she vowed. She summoned evil spirits and commanded them to raise a storm and sink the ship. But the ship's magic keel protected it against the queen's power.

"So Prince Richard comes prepared, does he?" the queen said scornfully. "Let us see if he can best his own sister." Nine times nine she passed her arms before herself, and three times three she chanted her spell. And when she was done, the Loathsome Dragon came down from the Spindle Stone to do her bidding.

The dragon slipped into the harbor and trapped the ship within its coils, holding it offshore.

"This beast cannot be Margaret," thought the prince, "for she would never oppose me so." Three times he attempted to land, and three times the dragon stopped him. Finally, he ordered his men to bring the ship about and head out to sea, even though he had but one day left to break the spell that bound his sister.

The queen laughed triumphantly. "So much for brave Prince Richard," she said. "Princess Margaret will remain the Loathsome Dragon forever!"

Prince Richard, however, had not retreated. He had anchored the ship in a hidden cove and was making his way on foot to the Spindle Stone, where the dragon lay once more. Still not believing that the ferocious beast could be Princess Margaret, Prince Richard rushed forward, his sword upraised. But he stopped short when he heard his sister's voice coming from the dragon's jaws.

Oh, quit your sword, forget your fear,
And give me kisses three,
For though I am a loathsome beast,
No harm I'll do to thee.

Prince Richard stayed his hand, not knowing what to think. Was this witchery too? Again the Loathsome Dragon spoke.

Oh, quit your sword, forget your fear,
And give me kisses three.
If I'm not changed by set of sun,
Then changed I'll never be.

"Surely this is the most monstrous creature I've ever seen," thought the prince. "Yet, just as surely, it speaks with my sister's voice." With firm resolve, he bent toward the beast, and once, twice, thrice he kissed its fearsome head. With a hiss and a roar, the Loathsome Dragon collapsed to the ground, revealing fair Margaret within its heart.

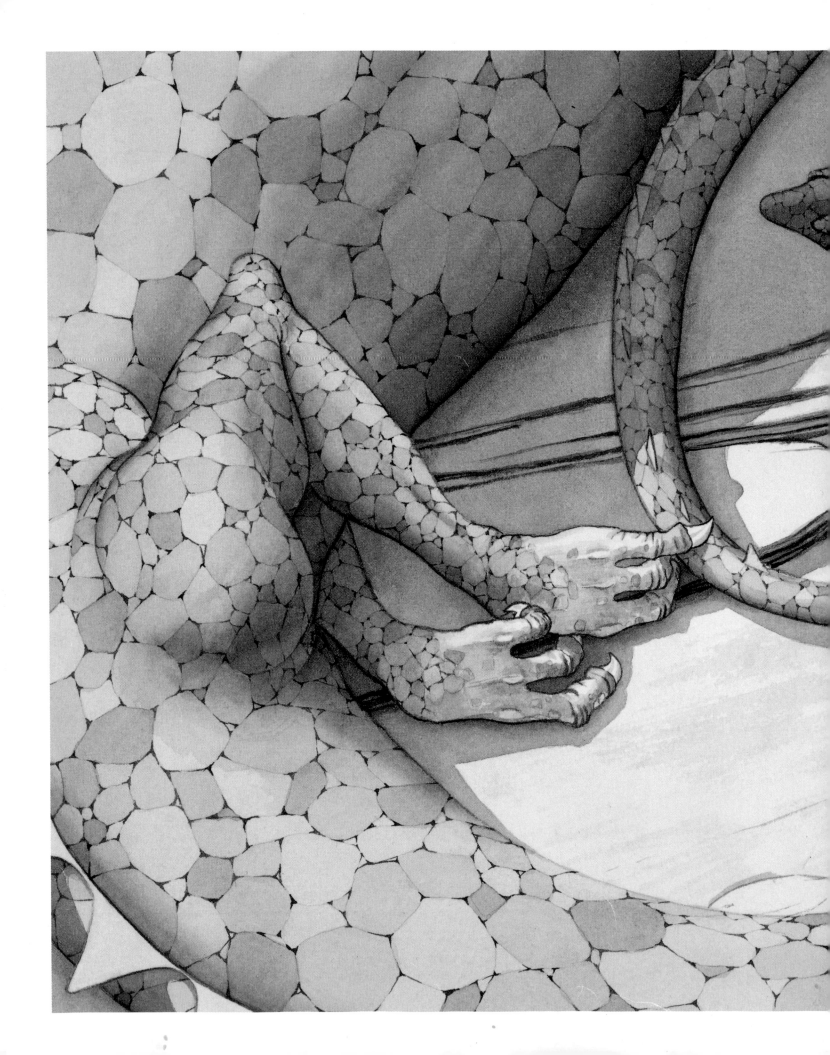

Together, sister and brother returned to Bamborough Castle. As they entered the main hall, the queen froze in disbelief. Prince Richard drew forth a rowan twig. A single touch, and the queen slowly shriveled into a Loathsome Toad. Croaking and hissing, it hopped away down the castle steps.

Free of the queen's enchantment, the king returned to his senses. He ruled the land with Prince Richard and Princess Margaret at his side, and all lived happily ever after. But to this very day, the Loathsome Toad haunts the grounds of Bamborough Castle, croaking in dismay whenever it catches sight of its reflection.